W9-BAH-654

FAIRIES from A to Z

A FAIRY BOX BOOK

APRIENNE KEITH

ILLUSTRATED BY WENDY WALLIN MALINOW

A SWANS ISLAND BOOK

TRICYCLE PRESS
Berkeley, California

Text copyright © 1994 by Adrienne Keith
Illustrations copyright © 1994 by Wendy Wallin Malinow
Swans Island Books, Sausalito, California ☺
With thanks to Shellei Addison of Flying Fish Books

TRICYCLE PRESS
P.O. BOX 7123
Berkeley, California 94707

Book and cover design by Wendy Wallin Malinow

Library of Congress Cataloging-in-Publication Data

Keith, Adrienne
    Fairies from A to Z / Adrienne Keith; illustrated by Wendy Wallin Malinow.
        p. cm. – (A Fairy Box Book)
    ISBN 1-883672-10-4
    1. Fairies–Juvenile literature. [1. Fairies. 2. Alphabet.] I. Malinow,
    Wendy Wallin, ill. II. Title. III. Series.
BF1552.K45 1994
[E]– dc20– dc20   94-2142
[398.21]   C1P
                                                                 AC
First Tricycle Press printing, 1994
Manufactured in Singapore   3 4 5 6 7 8 - 98 97 96 95

To my daughter, with whom I rediscovered the fairies; my brothers, who loved a cinnamon fairy long ago; and my husband, for believing.
—A.K.

To Ken
—W.W.M.

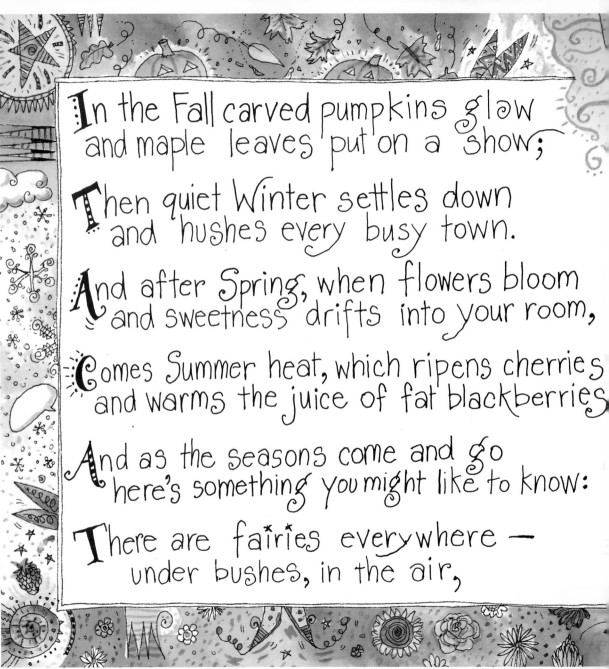

In the Fall carved pumpkins glow
and maple leaves put on a show;

Then quiet Winter settles down
and hushes every busy town.

And after Spring, when flowers bloom
and sweetness drifts into your room,

Comes Summer heat, which ripens cherries
and warms the juice of fat blackberries

And as the seasons come and go
here's something you might like to know:

There are fairies everywhere —
under bushes, in the air,

Dancing in the deepest woods,
  hiding out in neighborhoods,

Playing games just like you play,
  singing through their busy day,

Thinking thoughts and dreaming dreams
  in deserts, caves, and rocky streams.

Even up in outer space
  shooting stars and fairies race.

So listen, touch, and look around—
  in the air and on the ground—

And if you watch all Nature's things
  you might just see a fairy's wings.

air

accordion

Etching things a frosty white,
fairy ARTISTS paint the night.

Tea is served in an ACORN cup:
tip it gently, sip it up.

abuzz

butterfly

A BANDAGE made from flower petals cools the sting of prickly nettles.

Fairies living in a BOG enjoy the pearly haze of fog.

birthday

beautiful

B

COMETS streak across the sky
to light the way when fairies fly.

COCOONS spun of magic thread
make a warm and cozy bed. zzzzzzzz

castle

crown   camp

D

dance

dive

Fairies take their **DEWDRIP** showers
beneath the early morning flowers.

A pinch of fairy **DUST**, fine as powder,
is magical in seashore chowder.

delicate

dragonfly

delicious

feather

FiREFLiES, softly glowing,
light the night for fairy rowing.

Speckled FISH with shimmery scales
give rides to fairies on their tails.

friend

fun

G guitar

To call the fairies home for tea a treetop GONG is rung at three.

glass   ginger   gulp

golden

Fairy **GLOVES**, sewn with shells, are worn when casting water spells.

GARDEN fairies, planting seeds, love flowers, fruits, and even weeds.

guess?

giggle

A HAMMOCK made from seaweed string is hung from driftwood as a swing.

Fairies always HUG good-bye as they're taking off to fly.

hummingbird

A heather **HAT** worn in a storm
will keep a *fairy* dry and warm.

holly

heart

home

Fairies living where it snows build small **IGLOOS** for their toes.

invisible

iris

instrument

ivy

Some fairies dream of distant lands
with ISLANDS pink from coral sands.

insect

When the paths are slick with ICE,
fairies scurry 'round like mice.

icicle

imagine

JUGS of cream to start the day are bottled at the Milky Way.

Ladybugs, so small and round, are like bright JEWELS upon the ground.

joy

jolly

juggle

jingle

jubilee

kangaroo

Fairies always carry KEYS
to open shells and trunks of trees.

In the early morning hours
leaf KAZOOS wake up the flowers.

kiss

kite

king

kettle

k

listen

Rose-stem **LADDERS**, with steps of thorn lead to where rosebuds are born.

Fairy **LAUGHTER**, light as bubbles, chases off most cares and troubles.

HA! HA!

leaf

lily

love

merry

When sleeping under soft **MOONLIGHT**,
fairies dream all through the night.

Fairies brew a MEADOW stew
with stems and rocks and muddy goo.

mask

mirror

magic

m

Shells from NUTS of different sizes
are filled by fairies with surprises.

Whenever fairy NEIGHBORS meet,
they shake each other's hands and feet.

nod

night

nectar

noodle

N

Fairies sail the OCEAN skies
upon the backs of butterflies.

If a leaf is folded right
an ORIGAMI bird takes flight.

oak

orchid

oh!

octopus

Fairies often roll their curls
with pretty little OYSTER pearls.

ostrich   otter

PUDDLE PIE is easy to make,
add sand and grass, stir, then bake.

When fairies close their eyes at night,
Pussywillows feel just right.

peppermint

P

pinecone

prance

party

quest quiet

To write a letter in wet sand
take a feather **Quill** in hand.

Beneath a **QUILT** of glowing threads,
fairies lay their sleepy heads.

quick

queen quartz

rabbit   reindeer   rock

Deep among the oak tree **ROOTS** fairies hide their winter boots.

Fairies like to sink their noses into sweetly scented **ROSES**.

read

rest   robin   R

sun   sunflower

Fill a SANDWICH with ocean spread
squished between sand dollar bread.

starfish

sassafras

ahhchooo!

Wishes floating on the breezes
come from dandelion SNEEZES

On speedy SLEDS made out of bark
fairies race across the park.

slipper

shell

teapot

tickle

♪ Singing out in croaky tones,
TOADS give concerts on the stones.

TURTLES often sit quite still
if a fairy needs a hill.

When night owl hoots his TUNE
fairies dance beneath the moon.

tumble

treasure

tricycle

T

UMBRELLAS made from lily flowers keep fairies dry through spring rain showers.

For winter chills that freeze the air fairies knit long **UNDERWEAR**.

unicycle
ukulele
uncover
universe
uplift

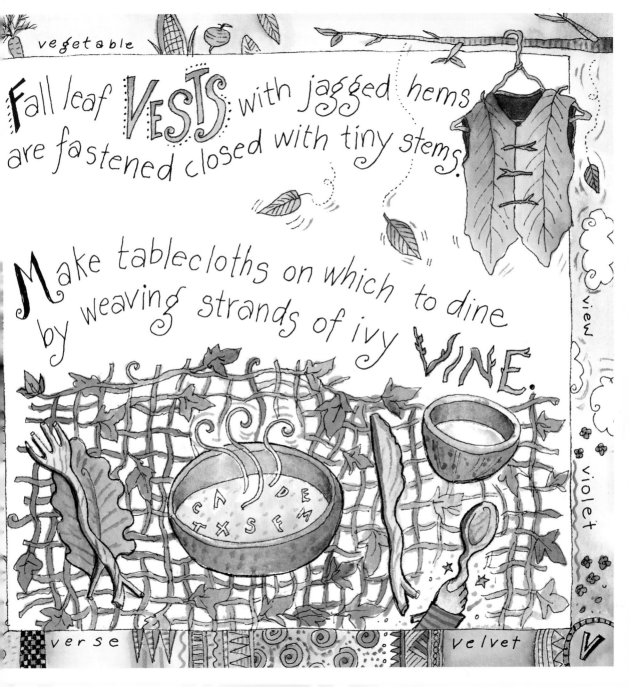

Fall leaf **VESTS** with jagged hems
are fastened closed with tiny stems.

Make tablecloths on which to dine
by weaving strands of ivy **VINE**.

vegetable
view
violet
verse
velvet

V

Fill **WALNUT** beds with dreamy stuff,
like petals, moss, and cotton fluff.

web

Dipped into a starry night, fairy **WANDS** twinkle bright.

A blade of grass used as a **WHISTLE** calls a fairy from the thistle.

word

wink

sweet roses

budding bushes

peapod boat

fairy box

deepest woods

pussywillows

tiny fort

fairy box

dusty desert

empty nests

X marks the spot on this map where fairies stop to take a nap.

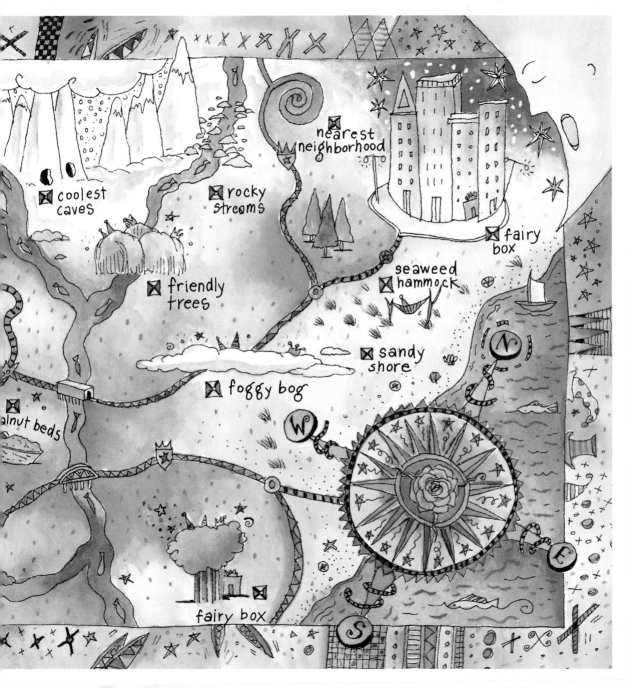

Toast with honey warms the tummy – fairies find it very YUMMY.

In the early light of dawn fairies stretch their wings and YAWN.

Year

Y

yipee!

you

yard

yak

yes!

When fairies **ZIP** from here to there,
sparkles linger in the air.

Fairies catch some morning **Zzzzz**
in the arms of friendly trees.

zebra

Every creature lives somewhere—
upon a leaf, inside a pear.

Birds stay snuggled in the trees;
hives are for the honeybees;

Bugs curl up against the rocks;
but fairies like a FAIRY BOX:

You know the things that please them most,
like walnut beds and honey toast,

So if you'd like a tiny guest,
build a cozy place to rest.

And if you see some magic things,
like glowworms, stars, and glistening wings,

You'll know a fairy's come to stay
to share with you the fairy way.